ROB DELPLANQUE

Echoes Of Reality

First edition

Cover art by Manav Khadkiwala

This book was professionally typeset on Reedsy.
Find out more at reedsy.com

For Holly.
My touchstone.
Forever grateful to have found you in this reality.

"You think that's air you're breathing now?"

– Morpheus, The Matrix

Chapter 1

It's a time of sterility here in 2132. Architectural behemoths of concrete and steel house the remnants of humanity, shielding us from the radiation that leaks like poison through the fractured wound of the broken sky that we alone created.

We rarely venture outdoors anymore, and when we do, it's under strict orders to limit the exposure to a matter of minutes.

Our focus resides on the inside.

The inside, looking out.

Too afraid to explore the stark nature of our world we instead focus on what remains in our control. Technology. And that has driven the development of *The Simulation*.

In the last generation alone it has come on leaps and bounds.

There are myriad reasons for building a simulation of life, but the main motivation in my mind is that it gives us an opportunity to save ourselves from this self-imposed isolation.

A view of a fictional world?

One better than our own?

That can give us an escape.

At least temporarily.

I first entered the simulation on the 15th of July, 2132. I have a tattoo at the top of my back to mark the occasion.

My name is Julius.

It's a Roman name; or so my father told me.

When I made the decision to get the tattoo, a friend said that I should put the date in Roman Numerals to honour my namesake. I'd never even heard of Roman Numerals before and why would I have? It's not like they're commonplace in the 2100s.

My friend Demetri wrote down the numerals: MMCXXXII. The enigmatic and rustic look of the block capitals appealed to me.

Although I had no idea if these characters actually meant 2132, or if he was fucking with me, I trusted him. It could have been some ancient Sanskrit for 'fuckface' for all I knew, but hey, the tattoo looks cool.

I'd spoken to a few people that told me they had entered the simulation. They'd all waxed lyrical about it; said it was the most amazing experience of their lives.

That's all I needed to hear.

Their words had implored me to put myself forward to trial it and a few days after getting inked — and the skin having healed — my day had come.

Until now I'd been on the periphery, waiting with baited breath for a time when I might get a chance in the *seat*. I'd read everything I could get my hands on about the intricacies of the simulation: how it had been developed; how many people had worked on it, and for how long; how detailed it was; what the purpose of it was; what the setting was. I was hooked by the idea — the sheer grandiosity of the project and the prospect of the escapism it offered from this world was awe inspiring.

"Julius?" said Mensch.

"Yeah?" I said, looking up to meet his gaze. I'd been lost in a daydream; fantasising about my upcoming trip into the unknown.

"You ready for this?"

"I've been ready for years. I was born for this," I said, feigning confidence.

His gaze lingered, searching my face. "I mean, are you *really* ready? This isn't like one of those games you like to play from a hundred years ago, you know? This is a whole other league. It's not... it's not for the faint of heart."

Mensch had a kind soul; a father figure to me and old enough to be so. He'd always had my back and I felt the sincerity in his voice and in his still, mellow, green eyes.

"Yeah, I'm ready," I insisted, my hands trembling. I focused squarely on Mensch's gaze. "I've done everything I can to prepare myself for this and now it's my turn. Get me in that seat before I change my mind."

Mensch proceeded to check my vitals and strap me into the seat. A neck restraint kept my head still, while bands were clasped around my wrists and ankles securing them tightly, yet comfortably, to the arm and leg rests.

As the restraints clicked into place a cold sweat broke out on my forehead. The room seemed to grow quieter; the ambient hum of the equipment fading into the background with an eerie shallowness. My heart reverberated in my chest; each beat, a drum, signalling the approach of an unknown future.

"Ok, my friend," said Mensch. "Your vitals are fine. Blood pressure is a little high, but I'd put that down to excitement... Or nerves. Both are sides of the same coin when you think about it." Giving my restraints a tug, he continued. "You're all strapped in. I just need to attach the nodes to your temples and then put the sensory deprivation gear over your eyes and ears." He checked my expression. His eyes, narrowed. "Then you're all set; I'll power up the simulation and you're off to dreamland. How are you feeling? Any questions before we kick this off?"

I gulped. The swell of anxiety, causing my mouth to go dry and my throat to tighten.

Is this gonna hurt?

"How am I *feeling*? I'm fucking buzzing... yet... terrified. How were you feeling on your first time? There... there *was* a first time for you, yeah? You have... you have done this before haven't you, Mensch?"

He paused. A look glazed over his eyes and my mind moved into overdrive as I attempted to pick up on exactly what this was.

Shame? Guilt? Concern?

"I haven't. I'm just the operator. I'll get my chance, no doubt. But you've pipped me to it, Julius."

"Oh, man. I didn't realise. I don't know... I... I just assumed that you'd been through this." If my neck hadn't been restrained I would have hung my head.

"I've facilitated a number of these, but my contract doesn't allow me to actually go into the simulation." His look was clearer now. One of quiet resentment. "Not yet at least. But maybe someday." He raised his eyes up to the ceiling with a far off, daydreamy stare.

"Mensch?" I said. He'd been quiet for a solid ten seconds. "Are we going to do this or not?"

Mensch shook his head, snapping back to the moment. "Yeah... sorry... I'll just grab the last bits."

Mensch trudged away and returned promptly with the necessary peripherals.

"Here we go," Mensch said, as he attached the nodes to my temples with a wet gel; the coolness sending a shiver up my spine and triggering goosebumps on my strapped down arms.

He brandished a couple of dark optical discs, custom sized to fit my ocular cavities, and a pair of ear plugs. "Anything else you want to mention before we start?"

So many questions, but so diffuse that I was unable to distil them down to coherent words. I could only vocalise one pathetic question that I knew he couldn't answer.

"How should it feel?"

Mensch looked as though he, too, was unable to distil his own thoughts into an effective response.

"I can't really say... As you know, I've never done this before. *You* bring me back that answer, ok?" Mensch's brow was furrowed with an intensity that matched his stare and his eyes glistened with a moistness that spoke volumes.

The excitement turned to full-on anxiety. Beads of sweat trickled down my shivering spine.

I shook myself in an attempt to fight the nerves; not wanting to give Mensch any sign that I might be on edge.

"Ok, let's do this. When I'm back I'll let you know how it was." Just saying the words caused my pulse to spike. "Boot me up."

Mensch nodded, his concern clear as day in his raised eyebrows. "Good luck," he said softly, as he applied the discs to my eyes and inserted the ear plugs.

Darkness.

Silence.

Stillness.

The only sensations - my drum of a pulse, the rapid rising and falling of my chest and the cold feel of the sweat running down my back.

My breath echoed in my ears. My inhales, sharp. My exhales, a whisper.

Whispers of fear.

Then.

A sensory void.

My body tightened; every muscle contracting at the speed of light.

I shuddered; convulsed as my mind was instantly filled with a million vivid images. Canvases of stills, yet cycling through at an unfathomable amount of frames per second.

A kaleidoscope of sensory input.

My consciousness was being stretched. Splintered.

I felt absorbed.

Entirely.

Falling into a cascade of infinite sensations.

And then....

Chapter 2

Hayden checked her reflection in the mirror. She'd always considered herself to be a solid seven, but this morning, she was delighted to see a definite nine staring back at her. There was a sparkle in her vivid, blue eyes. A lack of bags underneath them and a freedom in her expression. Her perfect smile radiated a lightness. To top it off, it was definitely a good hair day.

Seeing herself looking so good, so healthy and happy, gave her a tangible confidence boost. Just the jolt she needed on a day when she had a big date lined up that evening.

"Lock up your sons," she said aloud, as she pursed her lips and gave her mirror stare a kiss.

Hayden took a glance at her Casio wrist watch - 7:45 - still plenty of time before she needed to get to the office. She was particularly impressed with herself; she'd already had a 45 minute gym workout, a healthy breakfast and she'd showered and straightened her flowing blonde hair.

Her body felt deliciously tight. Her physique was on point, with curves and tone perfectly showcased under a denim skirt and black vest top.

She was on fire.

Grabbing her coveted Christian Dior saddle bag, she made her way out of her fifth-floor New York apartment and into the city streets.

Hayden was early. She had time to kill before work, so she took the scenic route via the walkway along the Hudson River.

The blue sky had the effect of over saturating everything around her. The hues were vivid. The clouds — of which there were few — were a cotton white, the trees, an ethereal green and the river a hazy blue. Colours so rich that the day had a surreal quality that she didn't normally associate with the often drab setting of New York City.

As she veered from the river path, she took the opportunity to stop at her favourite cafe that was just a few minutes walk from her office.

"Vanilla latté to go?" said Brenda.

"Am I that much of a regular that everyone knows my order here?" Hayden laughed.

"I think you know you are. Not a day passes that you don't come in here and order one. At *least* one."

Hayden routed through her saddle bag and pulled a handful of half-full loyalty cards, some of which were old branding. She felt her skin prickle as she turned a shade of red.

"I must be due a free one with all these stamps, don't you think?"

Hayden handed over her antique collection of loyalty cards and Brenda consolidated them.

"Here. You now have three complete cards and change, so this one's on the house."

"You're a doll. Thanks..."

"Brenda."

"Of course. *I* know." She didn't.

Hayden relinquished one of her loyalty cards in exchange for the coffee, thanked Brenda and left, her stomach knotted slightly from the shame she felt at not remembering her name.

Back outside, Hayden took a deep breath of the metropolitan air, exhaled sharply and took a sip of her vanilla latté; even that had an otherworldly tang to it. Her taste buds effervesced with the bitter sweetness and her nostrils were aflame with the aroma of the roasted beans and vanilla scent.

My word, that's good.

With a caffeine-fuelled pep and a spring in her step, Hayden strode towards her office, but first stopped at a newsstand to peruse the papers and magazines. A copy of the New York Times mentioned Billy Idol having been admitted to hospital for a drug overdose.

Hayden's eyes rolled.

These fucking rockers.

She still hadn't gotten over Kurt Cobain's suicide and had no sympathy for aging rockstars still overdosing on drugs as if it was fashionable and edgy.

Glancing away from the Times, she continued scanning and was drawn to last month's edition of Vogue magazine — July 1994. A typically tanned Cindy Crawford took up the entire cover's real estate — dressed in a short, yellow, sequined dress and clutching what Hayden assumed to be a blue beach towel.

She picked up a copy, paid the three dollars and continued her stride to the downtown office.

Up three floors in the lift, she entered her office floor through a pair of glass double doors and was greeted by Naomi on reception.

"Morning Hayden! I see you've got your vanilla latté there.... Oh, and what is that? The latest Vogue?" said Naomi, bright as a button, as per usual.

"Hey, Naomi. Yeah, you know me. I can't function without my morning caffeine boost. And yeah, it's Vogue. I'll lend it to you once I've skimmed through it."

"Please do. Thanks, honey."

Hayden moved through the office, conducting the usual, ritualistic meet and greet of her fellow coworkers and suffering the inane water-cooler chit-chat that was the mind numbing existence of the modern day office worker in the early 90s.

Having had a typically banal, quick catchup with everyone, Hayden scuttled off to her desk, clicked her computer monitor on and checked her in-tray for her latest fax communications.

She sipped the remnants of her latté as she absorbed the latest feedback from her editor.

There were a *lot* of red pen annotations on this latest fax, which caused Hayden's heart to race. Her deadline was looming and she'd hoped there'd only be a need for minor adjustments on her latest piece. One saving grace, however, was that something sent by fax turned everything to monochrome.

The red pen didn't have as much power these days.

She sighed, opened the file and began clacking away on the instructed refinements.

A welcome reprieve came when Izzy - Hayden's closest office friend - stopped by her desk with lunch for the pair of them. They retreated to the communal kitchen area and Izzy set down two falafel salads.

Hayden tucked in, popped a can of Diet Coke and slurped down a chunk of falafel that was having a hard time inching down her throat.

"So, the big date tonight then?" said Izzy, slightly slurring, due to a half-chewed mouthful of salad appropriating her jaws. "So many questions... who is he? Is he good looking? Does he have a good job?" An errant piece of lettuce fell from her mouth while she was mid sentence. "Where are you going? What are you going to wear? Oh, and remember, he pays, ok?"

Hayden's eyes were wired; overwhelmed by this question-posing onslaught. "Woah, slow down, hun."

Izzy righted herself. "I'm sorry. I'm just... I'm just really excited for you. I know it's been a tough time for you, since you broke up with John." She paused to finish chewing and took a breath. "I'm glad you're ready to move on."

"Thanks, babe. Ok, let me tell you what I know about the guy, eh? And don't get too excited. I don't know much about him just yet."

Izzy put down her knife and fork and rested her chin in her hands. "Okay. Shoot!"

"His name's Brad. He's... he's a banker."

"A banker?"

"Yeah. On Wall Street."

"Oh, wow! So he's rich?"

"Maybe," Hayden laughed. "We're meeting at a bar in town and I've got a nice, new black dress to wear. A Versace."

"Slutty?"

"A little."

"I like it."

"And that's all I know really. I haven't even met him yet."

"So this is like a blind date?"

"Of sorts. A friend of a friend set us up."

Izzy's look of intrigue turned to that of concern.

"Well, you be safe, yeah. And I want to hear all about this on Monday morning. Also, not just a big date. A big month for you, too, eh? You're going to Woodstock '94, yeah?"

Hayden gave a daydreamy smile. "Yeah I cannot wait for that. I can smell the toilets and the mud already."

Izzy's look of intrigue returned. "I'm so jealous. I've never been to a festival before and certainly not one *that* huge. Who are you most excited to see?"

"There's loads, but Aerosmith on the Saturday and the Chili Peppers on the Sunday are the ones I absolutely cannot miss!" Hayden said, an effervescence in her voice.

"God, you're gonna have such a good time. I wanna hear all about that, too."

"Oh, you will. But. First things first. Let's see how this date goes."

* * *

So much neon.

Seriously, what is this place?

Hayden sidled up to the bar, caught the attention of a server and ordered herself a gin and tonic.

She sipped away as she perused the venue in the search for Brad.

There was a thrum in the air. An electricity. A vibe. It wasn't a nightclub by any stretch, but there was dance music playing at an ambient level that spun in the air and, without even realising it, Hayden was rocking back and forth in cadence.

She scanned the floor of the bar - a wide open space with a couple of dozen tables and booths of differing sizes; mostly filled with clientele in business dress, drinking cocktails of varying colours, shapes and lengths, most of which were decorated with a vast array of accoutrements.

A tingling tension in Hayden's stomach snapped her back to herself.

Am I feeling butterflies?

She hadn't been on a date since her long term relationship with John had ended six months ago and she'd forgotten the sensation of first date nerves. Her mouth felt dry and she took another sip of her drink in a futile attempt to right it.

Hayden continued to scan the bar for a sign of Brad; her eyes flitting around anxiously. Having never met him before all she had to go on was a photo that her friend had shown her. She knew to expect mid-length, brown, slick, side-parted hair and a broad-toothed smile. Dredging up that loose memory she scanned again, focusing on the entrance to the bar and as she did she clocked someone that may just fit the picture. As their eyes met the man smiled.

A broad-toothed smile.

It was Brad.

He strode over towards Hayden. A confidence and suaveness in his step.

"Hayden?" Brad said, as he approached.

"Yes. *Brad*?"

"That's me. Nice to meet you and sorry to have kept you waiting." Brad leant in for an embrace and an air-kiss on each of Hayden's cheeks.

"Oh, I haven't been waiting long," Hayden replied, blushing.

Before the two of them had begun any small talk, Brad caught the eye of a wandering waiter, raised his eyebrows, clicked his fingers and pointed at a vacant booth. The waiter responded by ushering the pair of them over.

Hayden's cheeks reddened further. The immediate assertiveness and sleaze of Brad stirred a wave of embarrassment within her. Her armpits began to sweat.

There's confidence and then there's arrogance. I hope it's the former with this guy.

Under the subtle, but direct lighting of the booth Hayden could see Brad's features a little more clearly. He was deeply tanned and even beneath his sharp, slim-fitted suit she could tell he was toned in one of those only-money-can-make-you kind of ways.

As the waiter walked away, Brad clicked his fingers again and hollered back in his direction. "Can we get some table service here?"

The waiter scuttled back to the booth.

"We'll have two dirty martinis."

"But I–"

"You'll love them," Brad insisted, acknowledging Hayden's attempted interruption by giving a fleeting glance in her direction before averting his gaze back to the waiter.

"Ok, sir," the waiter acknowledged, before turning and scurrying away.

"They do a great dirty martini here. Trust me."

Hayden felt unsettled at this misogynistic play. The mansplaining was in full swing and Brad was making a terrible first impression on her. Yet, strangely the assertiveness was attracting her in a way that she couldn't rationalise in her own mind.

"Ok, I'll look forward to trying it," Hayden conceded, trying her best to maintain a positive tone.

Aside from the swing of the ambient music that continued to play, an awkward silence hung in the air. Brad fiddled with his tie. Tightening it and pulling at it. Checking the knot for perfection. Hayden meanwhile sipped away at the remnants of her gin and tonic, her fingers tapping away at the glass.

Brad finally broke the monolithic silence. "So what is it you do, Hayden?"

"For work?"

"Of course."

"I'm a journalist," Hayden replied. A pride in her voice.

"Oh, really? The Times?" Brad seemed impressed. His eyebrows raised with intrigue.

"No, nothing like that. I write for a women's health magazine."

Brad's eyebrows lowered. His brow furrowed.

"Oh. So you're all about supplements and that new age trash?" He spoke with a clarity. An accuracy. Enunciation was clearly important to him.

Hayden's chest tightened.

What's wrong with writing for a women's health magazine?

In an attempt to try and justify her profession, she said, "It's not all about supplements. There's a lot about diet. Aerobics. Mindfulne–"

"Lift more. Run more. Be more. That's my philosophy," said Brad, interrupting her before she could finish her sentence. He showed off his broad-toothed grin again, raising his shoulders and arching his back.

This fucking guy.

Arrogance it is.

The waiter returned with the drinks, set them down and left them to it.

"Salud," Brad said, as he raised his glass to make contact with Hayden's. Hayden reciprocated, took a sip and gasped.

"Woah, that's strong," she said, her eyes watering.

"But it's good, eh?"

"A little strong for my taste... but you're right, it's good."

Brad extracted the skewer from his glass and proceeded to pull the olive into his mouth with his fat teeth.

"And you know what *I* do, right?"

"You're in banking, yeah?" Hayden sighed.

"Well, more than banking. Mergers and acquisitions, generally," said Brad, a smug grin plastering his deeply tanned, wrinkle-free face.

Is that supposed to impress me?

"And you enjoy it?" asked Hayden, already predicting what his response would be.

"*Enjoy* it? Well, I make a lot of money doing it."

Hayden rolled her eyes and took another eye watering sip of her martini.

"Money isn't everything, you know, Brad? Surely there's more to life than that for you."

Tilting his head to the side, he said, "What more is there? Why do people go to work, generally?"

"Well–" Hayden tried to speak, but Brad was keen to answer his own question.

"To make a living, right?" He leaned forward. "It's just that some of us make a better living than others. Would I do this if I didn't get paid for it? No. Of course not. I do love it though. I love the feeling that it gives me when I make a big deal come off. I love the paycheck that comes with that and I love the fact that I'm doing better than ninety nine percent of the population."

Oh, man.

Brad's talk of the loftiness of his career seemed a well rehearsed act that may impress some women, but it wasn't dazzling Hayden. The honest truth was that she couldn't care less. She was more a believer that the character of a man was far more important than money, status, their job or what car they drove.

Brad was falling way short on the character side of things so far.

As he paused for a breath and a sip of his martini, Hayden attempted to interject again. "But—" It was futile, as he cut her off with a wave of his hand to continue his diatribe. She lit a cigarette.

"And it gives me the opportunity that most don't get. If I want to jet off to a tropical island at a moment's notice I can do it. As long as I'm near a phone then deals can get done. If I want to go to a football game or baseball game I can get the best seats at the drop of a hat. If I want a cigarette..." Brad gestured at Hayden's pack on the table in front of him.

"Sure, go ahead."

Brad retrieved a cigarette, lit it, took a huge drag and continued. "Then I can do that. Oh, and thanks. And if I want backstage passes to see Bruce Springsteen this weekend then I can do that, too."

That was the first thing to come out of Brad's mouth that slightly interested Hayden.

"Really?"

"You bet."

"I'm going to Woodstock '94 next weekend. I love live music."

Maybe we'll have something in common?

"Camping?"

"Yeah."

Brad turned up his nose.

"You wouldn't catch me dead at something like that."

I guess not.

"How am I not surprised?"

The two of them sat and drank three more martinis. With each new order Brad would characteristically click his fingers to get attention and every time a waiter appeared it seemed to be the same guy. Apparently he wasn't put off by Brad's attitude and almost blissfully unaware of how he'd previously been treated. Brad's lack of grace had simply gone unchecked.

Maybe it was just me?

Maybe she was too sensitive to Brad's demeanour, Hayden had thought, although she concluded that this was all a part of working in hospitality; dealing with assholes came with the territory.

As the waiter departed — having set down their fourth martini — Hayden scanned the bar area and noticed there were four waiters on hand, moving from table to table, attending to the throng of patrons. Each looked the same. Not just similar. Not just the uniform. They *did* share a uniform, but there was something else. They all appeared to have the same haircut. Same cheekbones. Same nose. Same eyes. Same eyebrows.

Was it really the same waiter that served us every time?

Hayden shook the thought from her head and continued her insipid conversation with Brad, hoping that something positive may emerge if she steered away from a career-focused narrative.

"So where do you live, Brad?"

"Central Park South," he said, as he reached for another of Hayden's smokes; a smug grin plastered over his tight, tangerine face. "I've got a great view of the park from my tenth floor balcony. Wanna see it later?"

Of course he lives there.

"I don't think so," said Hayden. She could barely tolerate

another moment with this guy. "I have work in the morning, so I'll need to get back."

"Another time then?"

He really can't read the room, can he?

"Sure. Another time," she lied, feigning a smile.

Brad reached into his jacket pocket and retrieved some keys. "Can I at least give you a ride home?"

"Haven't you had a bit much to drink?"

"What? *These?*" Brad said, pointing to the empty martini glasses on the table. "These barely touch the sides." There he was again with the broad-toothed smile, but this time he added a wink.

As if this guy could get any more insufferable?

"Ever ridden in a Ferrari?" Brad added, with raised eyebrows.

I underestimated him. Yes. He can be more insufferable.

"Can't say that I have," said Hayden; her tone, dry.

"I've got my 456 parked outside. Come on, drink up and I'll give you the ride of your life."

Hayden checked the time on her watch - 11:30 - and glanced down at her feet.

Do I really want to walk back home, at this time, in these *shoes?*

I could get a cab, although... he'll just insist that he drives me home.

How bad can it be getting a ride with him? And it'll save me ten bucks.

Although Hayden wasn't interested in Brad, his unpalatable personality or the car that he drove, the drunken devil on her shoulder spoke for her.

"Ok, why the fuck not."

Brad downed the remaining drops of his martini, stubbed out his borrowed cigarette and clicked his fingers once more to get the attention of the waiter. He paid for the drinks — including a healthy tip — and stood up to leave without waiting for Hayden to finish her drink.

Hayden took a final sip — all the while being eyeballed judgmentally by Brad — got to her feet and followed him outside into the Manhattan air.

Night had taken over the city and it had come alive since she had set foot in the bar. It had been daylight when she entered and the contrast was palpable. The light of the city was now replaced by artificial hues. Neons and fluorescents. Yellow taxis blared by, with honking impatience. Drunken ramblers emitted incoherent expletives and profanities. Faces appeared more stern.

Hayden was actually grateful for the opportunity of a ride home.

With a '*beep*' a pair of headlights flashed, highlighting the location of Brad's Ferrari.

"Come on. She's right over here."

As Hayden approached the car she couldn't help but notice how immaculate it was. Polished to a high sheen. No signs of a scratch, dent or even minor imperfection. A world away from her beaten up Ford.

Brad gestured for Hayden to get in and she sidled up to the door and folded into the embracing, yet firm, leather bucket seat.

So much leather on show.

Brad got into the driver's side, started up the engine and revved hard.

The car howled like a wolf baying at the moon and Brad pursed his lips in appreciation.

Hayden cringed.

"Where do you live, Hayden?"

"West forty second?" She said it as a question, expecting to be judged, although she was very proud of where she lived and the life she'd created for herself. Nothing she'd said all evening had seemingly impressed Brad and she couldn't wait to get home and out of his sight.

"Ah, nice part of town. Not too far from me."

She was relieved that for once, Brad seemed to acknowledge her existence as someone that had any self worth whatsoever.

"Uh-huh," was all that she managed in response.

Brad put the car in gear and, with a screech of tyres on asphalt, he hurled it into traffic, slaloming from lane to lane and weaving in between vehicles at high speed, only slowing for the reddest of red lights. Hayden gripped the sides of her seat and dug her nails into the firm leather cladding.

Hayden had never seen a Ferrari before, let alone been in one and yet all of a sudden she realised that she was noticing them on almost every street they turned down. That in itself was surprising, but also the fact that she could make anything out at all was astounding, as the pace they were driving at and the inebriated haze she was in resulted in her vision being merely a blur of red and white lights streaking across her retinas.

Brad burst through traffic as he chased down a green light on the horizon; eager to catch it before it transitioned. He swerved dangerously close to a taxi and made it with microseconds to spare, spinning the car into a drift as he rounded a corner.

"Jesus, would you slow down?" Hayden pleaded. Her palms were sweating. Her knuckles, white.

As the car drifted, the force – combined with the moistness of her palms – caused her hands to slip from the grip that she had on either side of her seat, sending them splaying in the air.

"Don't you want to see what this baby can do?" Brad said with a laugh that was devoid of any warmth.

He wrangled the steering wheel, shifted down a gear and revved the engine to its limits, drifting around another city street corner.

"No! I don't! I just want to get home in one piece. You've had four... maybe five martinis for Christ's sake. Slow the fuck down!" she screamed, panic rising in her voice, her heart pounding in her chest like a timpani drum.

Brad's demeanour was not affected by Hayden's protestations and he continued to ride the accelerator.

"Don't worry. The cocaine keeps me sharp," Brad sniffed. "Just enjoy the ride."

Hayden was sobering up fast. Her hands were beginning to shake and she started taking in giant panic breaths. No words would form. Sharp intakes of air were the only thing her mouth was capable of.

Her eyes flitted from the road.

To Brad.

To the increasing speedometer.

Back to the road.

To the wing mirror.

Back to Brad's now maniacal expression.

The car entered another skid.

There was something different about this one.

Brad's expression was different. There was a struggle painting his broad-toothed mouth.

"Fuck!"

With a thump the car mounted a curb. A thud echoed as Hayden's head hit the roof. A screech of brakes. A centrifugal surge. A concrete mass ahead.

Impact inevitable.

Was it seconds, or minutes that she had blacked out for? She couldn't say. Dazed, Hayden looked up and saw that the car was crumpled up against the corner of a city highrise; steam hissing through the hood. She arched her neck to turn her head to the side.

A shooting pain.

Brad was wrestling with an airbag that had gone off in his face. His cheeks dusted with powder. Hayden hadn't had that luxury. She looked on, shaken, as he brushed the bag aside and clawed his way out of the car.

As he did, Hayden noticed a spark.

A fire.

It started to billow in front of her.

The engine was ablaze.

She tried to reach for the door handle, but her hands wouldn't move. They were pinned to the dashboard, as was her body.

"Brad! Help!" she screamed, her voice cracking.

He heard her. She knew he heard her, but he was unmoving; standing idly by as he looked on with a vacancy in his eyes.

Hayden smelled the burning first.

Then she felt it.

Flames were starting to lick through the footwell.

She could smell the burning of rubber.

The soles of her shoes?

Then an agonising intensity of heat. A searing pain, as the flames set her feet ablaze.

She screamed. A raw, primal shriek that tore through the night. She stomped her feet futilely in an attempt to put out the fire that licked away at her lower body.

She looked over through the smoke-filled interior at Brad in the distance, expecting, *hoping*, that he would finally be coming to her aid, but to her horror he was edging away from the car. A panic in his eyes.

Powerless to move, Hayden watched on as the flames gripped hold. The pain was beyond anything she could understand. She could smell smoke, the burning of fabric, the burning of *flesh*.

Her consciousness was shutting off.

As the flames rose, she was taken over.

Engulfed.

Chapter 3

"It burns. It burns!!!" I screamed. "Brad! Brad, help me! It burns! I can't get out."

My neck. Restrained. Couldn't move.

My hands, also restrained.

My eyes, sightless.

I could feel the searing heat and I wrestled against what was holding me in place. My neck, straining, my hands, jerking.

I felt a hand reach out to grab my arm.

Brad?

Another hand pulled something from my ears.

Words; shallow at first.

"It's okay, Julius. It's *okay*."

Who's Julius?

A hand reached for my eyes.

I flinched.

Suddenly I could see.

A face. A face I knew that I knew, but I couldn't place.

Not at first.

"It's okay, Julius," the voice repeated.

"It burns!" I shouted, as the agony continued to consume me. "Who... who the fuck is Julius?"

"It's just your mind. You're not burning.... Look."

Suddenly my neck was free from any restraint. I looked down at my feet. They weren't burning. My body wasn't burning. But I didn't recognise it.

Where is my black dress?

Where are my heels?

Where's Brad's car?

Confusion throbbed through my mind. I panted. Gasped for air. Touched my chest with my now free hands.

Big hands.

Not my hands.

This doesn't feel like me. Too broad. Too flat.

"It's ok, Julius," the voice said again.

"Who the fuck is Julius? Why... why are you calling me Julius? I'm Hayden, for Christ's sake!"

I heard my voice and trembled as the sound of the words reverberated. Not recognising it coming from within me. Too deep. Too tenebrous. Not the tone of the woman that I knew myself to be.

A hand thrust a mirror in front of my face.

An ashen-skinned visage stared back at me. Grey. Pale. Sallow.

I shook. My chest tightened.

A stranger's face.

Although; somehow *familiar.*

I recognised the brown eyes. The tousled hair.

Then; the lips. The ears.

The cheekbones.

The tiny scar above my eyebrow.

I was Julius.

For several minutes I sat, wordless, taking giant inhales. Heaving in a man's chest that seemed capable of taking deeper breaths than I was used to.

Even after those desperate minutes of trying to come to terms with what had happened to me I found it hard to shake the intrinsic belief that I was a woman named Hayden.

As I remained in the seat the man who had brought me round sat, poised, on the floor by my side, watching as I breathed myself into a calm state. His compassionate gaze resonated with me and all of a sudden I knew who this man was.

"Mensch?" I said, my eyes moist.

A look of relief washed over his face. "That's right, Julius. It's me."

I blew air from my cheeks. "Woah. This is so fucked up. I'm Julius? You're sure I'm Julius?"

"For as long as I've known you, yeah."

My head was still spinning. Reeling. Words couldn't do my experience justice, but they were all I had and I used them to try and work through it.

"This is so strange. As much as I know within me that I *am* Julius... I also... I also know myself to be Hayden."

"What do you mean, exactly?" Mensch said, his brow furrowed. Clearly intrigued and perplexed by my statement.

"It's so hard to make sense of. So hard to... quantify." I pushed myself out of the chair and attempted to stand up. A wave of dizziness hit me and, stumbling, I collapsed into a cross-legged pose on the floor next to Mensch. "My rational brain is telling me... or at least trying to tell me that Hayden was part of the simulation. A *character* in the simulation, but... but she feels just as much a part of me, as *me*!"

Mensch looked on. He clearly had things he wanted to say,

but he didn't interrupt. His demeanour was calm. Supportive. I took a breath and continued in my attempt to distil my rambling mess of thoughts.

"I think I was in her world for maybe a day, but... it wasn't just that and... my god there's so much I can say about that. It's as though... although I might have been her for merely a day I had a whole... lifetime of memories. I *knew* her *life*!" Feeling breathless I paused to take a deep inhale and gather my thoughts. "I know her parents were called Steve and Nicky. I know she has a younger sister named Jessie who she doesn't talk to often enough and wishes that she lived closer to. I remembered her days of high school and high school isn't even a term I, as Julius, am familiar with.

"I knew that she grew up in a small farming community in Ohio and I've never even been to America, but... fuck... I know the country as if it was my own.

"I remember the bullies at school. The past boyfriends. I remember the friends. Such... such great friends. I remember my first fucking period for Christ's sake!

"I could feel her values and character traits. Some were synonymous with mine, but some were conflicting. I now have both in my brain. I can *feel* them. I have this mess of memories. Hers and mine. Both. Both at once." I took a deep breath and exhaled with a whoosh. "How long was I in her world?"

"Two minutes."

My eyes widened. My hands shook.

"Two minutes?!" I gasped.

"No bullshit. Two minutes. You can experience a whole lifetime in twenty four hours, as far as I know."

"Fuck."

I took a beat. Two beats.

"You know what else, Mensch?"

"Tell me."

"I know fucking roman numerals now."

Mensch laughed. "How about that!"

"I studied them briefly in junior high. I mean... Hayden did." I shook my head in surrender. "This is so freaky. I feel like I have two lives worth of memories in my head. In fact, hand me that mirror again, would you?"

Mensch passed me the mirror and I angled it so that I could see a reflection of my back. The reflection was reversed, of course, but even then I was able to make sense of it.

"MMCXXXII. Two thousand, one hundred and thirty two... Twenty one, thirty two."

"That's quite something, eh?"

I handed the mirror back and sighed. "Yeah, it really is. I can't tell you how amazing that experience was... *Is*!"

"What else do you remember? I want more details," said Mensch, salivating at the idea of learning more about my journey into the simulation.

I took a moment to look around. The industrial, technical and almost clinical setting that I found myself in was a far cry from that which I'd inhabited until a few minutes ago. The shimmer of that world was gone, yet I could still remember it with a vivid force. The overlapping memories of my two lives were overwhelming and I couldn't help but miss that world.

"I was in the nineteen nineties. Nineteen ninety four to be precise. I was a woman in her late twenties. A fantastic life. Living in New York. It was beautiful. I experienced walking along the river. A stunning river. I saw trees. I can still remember the names of the species. Birch. Oak. Poplar. Trees we don't even have here. Or maybe we did at that time, but don't now."

My mind was ablaze with the memories. Vivid memories. *Real* memories.

"I wasn't aware of being in a simulation at all," I continued. "It was so *real*. As real as me sitting here talking to you now. I knew how it felt to grow up in the nineteen eighties and the nineties. I guess I don't know how factually accurate it was though. Was it based on the actual history of this world? Could it be?"

"I don't know," Mensch said. He raised an eyebrow. "Do you remember any specifics that we can check out to see if they're accurate?"

"Kurt Cobain?"

"Who?"

"Cobain," I whispered. The memory resonated hard. I felt a pang in my gut. A lump in my throat. I could feel my sadness. No; *Hayden's* sadness for the death of this man. There seemed to be no distinction in my mind of where her feelings and memories started and ended and where my own began. "He was a rockstar in a band called Nirvana, apparently. I was a huge fan. I mean... Hayden was a huge fan. He killed himself in April, nineteen ninety four."

"I'll look it up," said Mensch, getting to his feet.

"I know their music."

"Huh?"

"I know it. As if I grew up listening to it. I know every drum beat. Every chord. Every lyric. I knew what it meant for a generation of teens growing up. The genre. It was classified as grunge. I know other bands, too. I'd never heard of any of this before, but Hayden knew this stuff. Now I do, too." I blinked. Flashes of her memories, whizzed behind my eyelids. My memories now, too. "I've lived her life and it was beautiful.

It's a part of me now."

Mensch quickly dialled up the info and began to reel off his findings, narrating to me in plain speech.

"Kurt Cobain. Frontman of grunge band Nirvana, formed in a small town in Aberdeen, Washington, became a powerhouse in the grunge movement that overtook the port town of Seattle in the early nineties," Mensch said, his eyebrows raised in intrigue. "Cobain took his own life with a shotgun blast to the head on— "

"Fifth of April, nineteen ninety four," I finished, catching a glimpse of shock on Mensch's face as I rattled off the fact from my alternate memory. I was sure the shock on my own face mirrored his. I was just as blown away knowing that my experience in the simulation was as historically accurate as the real world that I was inhabiting in this moment.

"Yeah," Mensch whispered.

"I know it. I remember it. I was devastated by the news when it landed. Or should I say Hayden w— "

My head throbbed.

I winced.

I felt a drip.

A crimson droplet fell and painted a small spot on the crumpled trousers of my cross-legged pose.

Another drip.

My head felt light. Dizzy.

"Julius. Your nose?"

I wiped a hand across my nostrils and a scarlet streak stained my index finger from knuckle to tip.

Another drip.

Several drips.

"Jeez. Put your head back," Mensch ordered.

Obeying, I tilted my head back as Mensch marched away and

returned with a cloth which he held to my nose, soaking up the blood that had littered my face.

"Are you ok?"

"It's just a nosebleed," I gargled.

"Do you have them often?"

I paused to consider. I can't remember having one since I was a kid.

Can I?

My stomach flipped as I realised that this wasn't a *me* memory. It was a *Hayden* memory.

As Julius, I can't consciously remember ever having a nose-bleed.

"I don't think so," I said in surrender, tilting my head forward to face Mensch. I wiped my nose with the cloth, the bleeding seemingly relented. "I'm fine."

"You sure?"

"Yeah, I'm sure. It's nothing," I said, mildly perturbed. "I want to go in again."

"In again?" Mensch looked confused.

"The simulation."

Mensch shook his head in detest. "I can't let you do that, Julius. Not yet. You've just been in and you've acquired a lifetime's worth of someone else's memories in just two minutes. Your brain must be exhausted from that. You need to rest." He gave me that sincere stare again and I knew that he was right. "Plus, that nosebleed has scared me. Go and sleep it off and we'll talk again in the morning, yeah?"

"Yeah, ok," I said, as I got to my feet. A wave of dizziness hit me again. I stumbled a little, but with a deep breath I managed to keep myself steady and hoped that Mensch hadn't noticed my slight uneasiness. "See you in the morning."

I traipsed away to my room and hit the bed with a thud.

I was asleep in microseconds.

* * *

I whirled in an ever ebbing dance. Back and forth, like waves crashing on a shore and being dragged back out by the riptide. I was liquid. Alive in that state. The dance took me from the confusing days of junior high to the dizzying drunken nights of college, then, surging violently back to the coming of age days of high school.

At peace there for a moment it flipped; merged into the dark days of isolated living, surrounded by the hum and warmth of machines.

Then.

Blue skies. The buzzing of machines, replaced by the natural warmth of a glowing sun, bathing my skin in its sheer beauty.

I walked in nature.

I was Hayden, but with my eyes.

Who was *I*?

I awoke with confusion. I reached for my bedside table, to check my wristwatch for the time, but there was no wristwatch; just digital screens. A field of information at my fingertips.

My eyes, struggling to deal with the dark, required precious seconds to adjust to the absence of light.

Recognition.

This was not New York.

This was not my fifth floor apartment.

I unsheathed myself from the blanket that covered me; looked down at my body.

I was Julius.

I wiped my nose and a crusting of dried blood flaked off onto my fingers.

The nosebleed.

Has my brain overloaded from this sensory experience?

The dreams had been vivid. Almost as vivid as the world I inhabited a day ago for what felt like a lifetime, yet was only two minutes.

My palms were sweaty and I shook. There was a primal fear in the realisation that I was a tangled mess of two people. One, illusory. One, real. One, a true life history. The other, a construction, but yet, such a beautiful construction. Far more real than real.

Hyperreal.

Unable to get back to sleep I got dressed, left my room and trudged back to the tech room; summoned by the machine hum.

I sat near the apparatus for hours, waiting patiently for Mensch to rouse and make an appearance.

My head no longer throbbed; my nose didn't bleed; but my mind still thrummed with the duality of personalities and life experiences that dwelled within. I was unsure about how I would deal with a third set of memories, but the simulation beckoned me. Like a junkie who was craving their next fix I was powerless to stop it's call. Now that I'd had a taste I wanted more.

Needed more.

"Julius?"

I turned to see Mensch; his eyes, puffy. Clearly he'd just

woken.

"Hey."

"What's up? Why are you sat there?"

I could tell that Mensch knew the answer to his own question and I was unsure about how to play this without coming across as some kind of deranged addict. I needed to play this down somehow.

"I was just reflecting."

"On yesterday?"

"Yeah. What else? It was quite a day."

"Life changing by the sound of it." Mensch looked concerned. My attempt at playing it down wasn't having the desired effect, but surely it was better than me just coming out and saying that I was ready to go in again. "How's the head? Did you sleep ok?"

"It's fine. I feel fresh." This wasn't a lie. I did feel fresh, but my mind was still busy. I didn't want to give Mensch any reason to push back on my going into the simulation again though.

"Glad to hear it. No more nosebleeds?"

"Not at all. Like I say. Fresh."

"Good. And how's the head? You still believe you're a woman named Hayden underneath it all?"

"No," I feigned a laugh. "Those memories seem to have faded." It was a clear lie, but Mensch's expression suggested that he accepted it as the truth.

A pang in my stomach.

Guilt?

"I had some vivid dreams though," I continued. This *was* the truth and you know what they say? A lie is most conveniently hidden between two truths. "Perhaps that was my mind's way of filtering my reality from the simulation."

"Yeah, I guess that would make some sense, eh?" Mensch

ruffled his hair, scrunched his eyes. "You know... I'm relieved. I was worried about you for a second."

"Me too. A little. But honestly I'm fine. I could go in again if you wanted me to," I said, handing the responsibility back to Mensch. I didn't want it to seem like I was dying to get back in that seat. I wasn't sure whether these simple mind games would work, but it was worth a shot.

"If *I* wanted you to?" Mensch said, his brow furrowed.

"Yeah. You know... if you wanted me to bring back more information from the simulation?"

Mensch stared at me. He was sizing me up. Looking for any sign of weakness in my resolve. I stared back; putting on my best poker face and managing to stifle a gulp.

"Ok, give me a few minutes to think it over. Do you want a coffee? I know I need one."

"Coffee sounds good," I said, without emotion.

As Mensch traipsed away I let out a sharp exhale, my hands shaking.

"Here," Mensch said, handing me a steaming cup of black coffee.

"Thanks."

"Ok, so here's the deal." My heart began racing. "I'll put you back in for a few minutes, but if you start freaking out or if your vitals spike I'm pulling you straight out."

A few minutes.

That's a few days *in paradise.*

I set my coffee down on the floor. My hands were trembling so much that I risked spilling it and giving away the excitement and craving I felt for getting back into that seat.

"Ok," I said, dryly. "I'd expect nothing less."

I was back in the seat.

The nodes; reattached. The neck and arm restraints, locked.

Like one of Pavlov's dogs, I was conditioned. The hum of the machines was causing me to salivate at the prospect of exploring one of these alternate worlds for a second time.

My mind was calm. Surprisingly calm. I was trying my best to remain fully focused on the present moment although the excitement of what was to come was palpable and I was powerless to stop it distracting me.

I took a breath.

Goosebumps.

Despite my neck being restrained I was able to side-eye Mensch at the control panel. I squinted to see more clearly and could make out the individual commands he entered to prepare the simulation.

I made a mental note.

He strode over to me with the ear plugs and ocular discs.

"We're all set, Julius. Remember, if I see anything that I'm not happy with I'm pulling you out immediately," he said, staring me down, clearly scrutinising my body language.

"You've always got my back... I appreciate it," I said, fighting to keep my hands from shaking - grateful for the fact that they were restrained. "Let's do this."

I almost called him *'babe'*. Not my words. Hayden's words. Fortunately I caught them before they spilled from my mouth.

"Ok."

Mensch inserted the ear plugs and placed the discs over my eyes.

The sensory deprivation heightened my senses.

I became aware of my pulse. Elevated. I could feel the incessant thumping in my chest; hear it pounding in my ears.

I took sharp inhales. Focused on them.
Then...
Lights.
Colours.
Flashes erupted behind my mind's eye.
My body. Rigid.
Time and space bending, stretching, into a new reality.
This world?
Gone in a blink.

Chapter 4

"London. You're beautiful," I murmured. "Good night!"

Consciousness.

Consciousness returning.

I was Hunter, saying goodnight to my crowd of baying fans as I retreated away and threw down my guitar on the sticky, beer soaked stage floor to the sounds of screams and chants.

No, I was Hayden.

No. I was Hunter.

No. No. I was Julius.

A hand reached for my eyes and removed what was restricting my view.

Another hand removed plugs from my ears; silence replaced by an ambient humming.

My eyelids flickered, focus betraying me for a second until the man became apparent.

"Do you know who I am?" the voice said.

Coming into view now; the fog clearing.

I knew.

"Mensch."

"Do you know who *you* are?"

I scrunched my eyes. Tried to wipe them, but then realised

my hands were restrained. I widened my eyes, blinked several times and stared at Mensch.

"Now that's the question, eh? I have so many memories. So many identities."

Mensch looked up to the ceiling in abandon.

"Don't worry, Mensch. I know I'm Julius." I wasn't sure of the words I spoke, but he looked relieved. "At the core, anyway. Not that I wouldn't prefer the identity I had until a few seconds ago."

Mensch's eyebrows raised. He licked his lips. "You've got to fill me in, man," he said, as he released me from my restraints and handed me a cup. "Here's your coffee."

"My coffee?"

"Yeah. Don't you remember? I made you a cup a few minutes ago."

"Huh? A few minutes ago?" I cradled the cup. It was still warm. "How long was I–"

"Just over four minutes."

My head pounded. I gasped.

"Fuck."

Four minutes?

"Although I guess that's a little over two days for you, right?"

Holding my coffee, I wondered whether Mensch was playing a trick on me. It made no sense that a coffee that as far as I was concerned was brewed over two days ago, in another life, was still hot.

"I'll never get used to this," I sighed. I took a sip of the still slightly steaming coffee and an otherworldly sense came over me. I'd acquired another man's life memories since this drink was brewed. My stomach flipped. "This is the definition of surreal, muchacho."

"Muchacho?"

"Yeah, muchacho," I repeated.

"Since when do you use the word 'muchacho'?"

I gulped.

Not my words.

Hunter's words.

"Fuck. Sorry. Must be a hangover from my time as Hunter."

"Hunter?"

I got out of the seat.

As though I was standing at the top of a tall building and looking over the edge at a street one hundred floors down, dizziness hit me. The periphery of my vision started to close in with a black swell that threatened to engulf me and arrest my consciousness.

I grasped the armrest of the chair for stability in hope that the wave of vertigo would pass. I focused on the background noise of the machine hum and took a couple of deep breaths.

The black cloud disappeared and my balance returned. Somehow I'd kept hold of my cup without spilling a drop.

I took a seat on the floor next to Mensch.

Déjà vu.

"You ok?" said Mensch, a look of concern etched on his furrowed brow.

"Yeah. Just... just a wave of dizziness, that's all." I patted my stomach and chest, in an attempt to ground myself in a sense of reality. "The re-entry does have a bit of a kick," I said, playing it down.

"Just relax for a bit. But, hey... '*muchacho*', tell me about your experience as this 'Hunter' guy."

I took a sip of coffee. My hands, visibly shaking and creating ripples in the cup as I held it tight.

"I was a fucking rock star."

"Huh?"

"Hunter. I was a rock star in a band. The year was twenty thirty four and I was the frontman in a band here in the UK. Or at least it was still the UK then. We were on tour and the crowds were heaving. It was a frenzy. A purely hedonistic time. Drink. Drugs. Girls. So... so many girls."

I looked at Mensch, his interest clearly piqued. His eyes wide. His nostrils flared.

"Keep going," he said.

"I was having sex with what they'd call 'groupies' every night. Such amazing sex. The rest of the band weren't so interested it seemed though. There was a culture of people having relationships with AI instead. That seemed to be the norm at that time. There was a population crisis as the rates of childbirth had declined so that for every person on the planet less than one was being born. There was fear that humanity would collapse.

"Humans were acting like pandas. And that's where it started it seems. It's definitely been a trend that has followed through and the population on Earth in *our* time is certainly nothing like it was in Hayden's world.

"I remember Hunter saying 'I felt like putting a bullet through the eyes of every panda that wouldn't screw to save its species'. Apparently a direct quote from his favourite movie."

"Which was?"

"Fight Club, I think it was called."

"Never heard of it."

"Me neither... Well not before this." *Had I?* "But Hunter had and now I have, too." I set my coffee down; unable to cope with the shakes. "Another stockpile of memories from another life."

"Must be overwhelming."

"To say the least," I said. "You know what else?"

Mensch's eyes twitched. He smiled.

"Enlighten me."

"I think I can play guitar now," I said, a gentle smile crossing my lips.

Mensch's mouth opened wide and his brow furrowed.

"You can, what?"

"Play guitar. I... I think."

Mensch's eyebrows raised and his eyes widened as he said, "I have a guitar in my room. Let's give this a shot."

"Really? Wow. Ok, go grab it. I'm as keen to know if this'll work as you."

"Ok, muchacho. Hold fire."

Mensch returned a couple of minutes later brandishing a guitar.

Clocking the guitar, I said, "That's a 60s Fender Stratocaster." The words spewing from my mouth came as a complete shock. I knew nothing about guitars, but Hunter clearly did. And now *I* did.

Could I really play this thing?

Mensch handed over the guitar.

I placed it in my lap. Stroked the fine alder body, caressed the strings. Familiarised myself with the instrument. My hands on the wood felt comfortable. Natural. Like coming home.

A second later my fingers were flying up and down the fret-board with the workmanship of an expert. I was playing arpeggios, scales, chord progressions and complex solos. None of it made any sense to me – Julius – but, to my adopted persona of Hunter, I was a master of the craft.

The shakes from my hands were gone, as *he* took over;

possessed by this alter-ego.

With a deep exhale, I handed back the guitar. My hands, steady. Mensch's hands trembled as he took it from me.

"This... is... *crazy*," he said, his voice shaking, as his eyes flitted from me to the guitar in confusion.

"You're telling m—"

A sharp crack went off in my mind.

Pounding.

Throbbing.

It felt as though my head was being squeezed in a vice.

I winced, but aware of Mensch's presence I tried my best to obscure the contortion in my face and hide my pain.

Fighting through the tightness in my head, I struggled to my feet.

"Are you ok, Julius?"

"Y... yeah. Fine. I... just need to go... to the bathroom."

Before Mensch could question me further, I scuttled off with a weave to my steps, past the drone of the machines which throbbed in tandem with my brain, worsening my symptoms as I made my way to the bathroom.

I barged through the door. The bang of entry caused my face to scrunch tight with pain and I looked at my ashen expression in the mirror.

The sight morphed.

Julius's face, merging into Hunter's, then into Hayden's.

An ugly conglomerate of all three identities stared back at me.

I shook my aching head to fight against the hallucinogenic vision and as I did a droplet of blood fell from my nose and into the sink below.

I ran the tap; cupped a palm-full of water and splashed myself in my colourless face. The shock of the fresh, cold water cleared my throbbing mind for a brief second.

Until.

Another drop.

Another.

The dam opened.

A torrent of blood began to stream from my nose.

In futility, I tried to wipe it away, but there was no stopping the incessant crimson flow.

I remembered Mensch's advice and tilted my head back, while tightly gripping the sink. My knuckles as white as my face. Camouflaged against the porcelain.

I felt the flow of blood trickle down my throat. Tasted the metallic tang.

As I held on, the black veil reappeared. My peripheral vision diminishing by the microsecond.

My grip on the porcelain relaxed.

Chapter 5

My hands felt the cool touch of ceramic.

Tiles?

My eyes blinked open and immediately squinted at the throbbing in my skull.

Where am I?

Disoriented and dizzy I pushed myself up, but my hands slipped on a sticky liquid and my face crashed back to the floor with a crack.

I nearly lost the battle with consciousness, but I managed to keep my senses in check through sheer determination and a few deep breaths.

Inhaling sharply, I secured my palms to dry spots on the floor and pushed myself up with a pronounced exhale. Struggling to my feet, I slipped as if I was walking on ice, but managed to maintain my balance – purely by instinct – by reaching out and clutching onto a surface in front of me that I couldn't yet see.

A shower of blinks and then I widened my eyes. The black void at the periphery of my vision ebbed away and brought focus to my surroundings.

I was in the bathroom.

Blood.

Everywhere.

The nosebleed.

I looked down at the sink. Spatters and clots of congealed blood coated the surface. The floor beneath me awash with streaks and pools of maroon.

My hands shook as they gripped the sink. A sweat broke out on my brow.

I looked at my face — *Julius's* face — in the mirror. A horror show. A goatee beard formed of dry, crusted blood.

I shuddered.

Panic was ensuing. I needed to hide this from Mensch. I took a few sharp intakes of breath, splashed my face with water and rubbed hard until the devilish goatee was washed clean.

I kept the tap running; mopped up the soaking blood in the sink with my trembling hands and watched as it formed a red, translucent whirlpool that descended through the plughole.

I splashed the floor and wiped up the remnants of the viscous liquid with mountains of toilet tissue and flushed them away.

A wave of relief hit me as I looked around the bathroom — the evidence of my nosebleed, a thing of the past.

I stared at myself again in the mirror and a thought made my head spin:

I've lived for over a hundred years, yet I, Julius, am only thirty two.

As I opened the bathroom door, the cool air of the corridor hit me, and I felt a momentary sense of relief. I put out an arm and rested it on the adjacent wall for support. My legs were jelly.

I took a deep breath, sighed it out and headed back to my room to sleep off the headache that still pounded.

On my way I passed Mensch.

"You, ok? You've been in the bathroom for a while," he said. The concern in his face was palpable.

"Oh... oh... yeah. Fine. Just... just a bit of a dodgy stomach. No big deal," I said, as I waved a hand dismissively. "I'm just gonna get a bit of rest." I didn't think Mensch was buying it and I was fully aware that this sounded like a lame excuse, so I forced myself into a strong posture. "Like last time, I think I just need to let the memories from this journey distil and fade away."

Like that's gonna happen.

"Ok. Just let me know if you need anything, yeah?"

"Sure. Thanks, Mensch," I said, as I scurried away with my head bowed and trying my best to avoid eye contact with my friend.

I fell onto my bed and pulled a blanket over me.

I looked up at the ceiling; a whirlpool of memories descended upon my spinning mind as I struggled to reach sleep. I remembered nights on tour as Hunter; my long dark matted hair, my muscular physique, my sweat-soaked t-shirts, my chaotic guitar riffs. Days and nights in New York; my long blonde locks, my toned body, my feminine wiles.

Memories veered into Julius's territory - growing up in the 2100s. The isolation, the bleakness, the lack of connection. The yearning for more.

Are these memories, or just lucid dreams?

As I tossed and turned, rallying against the overwhelming nature of the mixed and fabricated memories, the exhaustion took over and consciousness faded like dying embers.

I was swimming.

Erratic strokes.

Six legs. Six arms. Three hearts. A human octopus.

I woke.

Drenched.

My pillow, saturated. My brow, dripping. My sheets, sodden.

I pulled my blanket aside, shuddered and sat cross-legged on my damp mattress.

Wholly disoriented, I reached to my bedside table and tapped the screens for the time.

00:01.

I must have slept for twelve hours.

Reeling from my dreams and my head still spinning I sat for several minutes coming to terms with the events that had taken place over the last couple of days. I'd inherited two extra life time's worth of memories and my vivid dreams were merging my subconscious into one.

I'm Julius.

But I'm so much more than that.

The memory of the nosebleed and the blackout returned, but I shook my head in objection, trying to convince myself that it was nothing to worry about.

There was a stronger force at play.

A desire — one that overrode the doubt and anxiety; outweighed the throbbing brain that was inhabited by three personas.

I had a need to experience more, but my rational brain began to question whether I should. My mind was running overtime with existential questions:

Can my head cope with more memories?

Will my brain later dismiss the fake from the real and free up space needed for me to experience more?

If not... will this kill me?

There were clearly risks, but, with cognitive dissonance at play, I concluded that life in the simulation was infinitely more exciting than the mundane existence I was inhabiting outside of it.

The risks are worth it.

I stood up straight. Arched my shoulders back.

I had to go in again.

I had to go in without a curfew.

* * *

I snuck out of my room and, drawn by the faint machine hum, I carefully tiptoed towards the technical area; muted fluorescents lighting the way as I strode with purpose along the steel gangway.

As I entered the control area, the sight of the vast, dimly lit room and the droning hum of the machines caused me to shudder. There was an eeriness to this space at night that was tangible and my skin pricked with suspense and wariness. My legs began to shake and I steadied myself by grasping a handrail and taking a breath.

Finally composed, I wandered to the control panel and reflected on my memory of watching Mensch input the parameters. I scanned the screens and familiarised myself with the controls and attempted to replicate his prompts.

The faint hum rose to a higher frequency as the system obeyed my inputs.

My brow broke out in a light sweat.

I continued tapping away. My technical skills were adept, but this was new territory for me. I wasn't familiar with this interface, but I seemed to be getting the desired response. Was this luck? Intuition? Or was it just that I'd paid more attention to what Mensch was doing than I'd realised?

I hesitated.

My chest tightened as I realised that I had no way of knowing the impact of starting the simulation without me being present in the chair. I took a breath and scanned the parameters in further detail. Despite my technical prowess there were many I couldn't decipher – names of myriad variables were listed whose intentions weren't obvious to an imposter like me.

My head dropped in abandonment.

I shouldn't be doing this.

I looked back to the screen in acquiescence, preparing myself to cancel the prompts I'd already entered; resigning myself to having to go back to my room and cut my losses.

As my finger hovered over the controls I noticed one parameter I did understand.

My eyes widened.

The electricity of goosebumps swept across my flesh.

A countdown.

I can trigger a timer before the simulation kicked in.

The fluorescent lights above me flickered and I took a beat as the angel on my shoulder piped up:

You can change your mind, Julius.

You know this is a risk, right?

When you were Hayden you believed you were burning to death. If Mensch hadn't pulled you out would your mind have made that a reality for you?

What if you're forever trapped in the simulation? What if Mensch finds you too late?

The illusion of free will was quickly shattered and I tapped away, setting a thirty second delay. I grasped the sensory deprivation gear and raced over to the seat, counting down from thirty in my mind.

The sounds of the machines ramped up. More of a roar than a hum now.

I applied the gel and plastered the nodes to my temples, inserted the ear plugs and positioned myself in the chair.

I estimated there were ten seconds remaining.

A chill swept over my body and a cold sweat crept down my spine.

I couldn't secure myself in the restraints without assistance, but dismissed this as an unnecessary factor and composed myself with a few deep breaths, slowing my kick-drum of a heart.

As I placed the discs to my eyes my senses were attacked with the relentless onslaught I'd come to expect. My body convulsed with infinite stimulus.

Just once more, Hayden.

*No...*Julius.

Behind my mind's eye fragments of consciousness splintered in a million directions as the simulation kicked in.

My brain was being stretched once more and I was powerless to stop its stranglehold.

Chapter 6

18/08/1972

Daryl sat in the docks, waiting for his judgement to rain down; his head bowed and his hands shaking. His unkempt brown hair was slick with sweat and his ashen, dishevelled face looked hollow and lifeless.

The courtroom sat silent. Waiting. A thrum of expectation hung in the air.

The judge was poised. Stone-faced, as he shuffled papers at the bench and cast a stern stare at the defendant.

"Mr Daryl Jackson, please stand."

This foreboding statement broke the silence with a colossal weight. Daryl gulped and pushed hard against his heels to raise his body from the wooden chair that had made his buttocks numb from the last few hours he'd sat there in silence.

His body had never felt so heavy.

A sweat broke out on his trembling back and a chill ran through his veins, as he looked up to meet the steely gaze from the judge.

"Mr Jackson."

As the judge began his sentencing, Daryl silently prayed that he might not be proven guilty for his crimes, but his conscience knew better.

This might be your last moment as a free man.

Detached, he couldn't even think of himself in the first person.

"You have been found guilty by a jury of your peers of the most heinous crimes: the brutal rape and murder of four young women."

The floor seemed to give way beneath Daryl, and he clutched the table for stability.

"The evidence against you has been overwhelming, and yet you have shown no remorse for the unspeakable pain and suffering you have inflicted on the victims, their families, and the community.

"Your actions are beyond comprehension. You took the lives of four young women, each with their own hopes, dreams, and futures, in the most brutal and callous manner. The impact of your crimes will be felt for generations, leaving a scar on the lives of all those who knew and loved these young women."

The judge's words were a barrage to Daryl's senses and as he rained the judgement down upon him Daryl side-eyed the jury. All members glared at him with the same expression; a mix of disdain, disgust and condescension.

"The court has considered the appropriate sentence carefully, weighing the aggravating factors, which are numerous, against the complete absence of any mitigating factors. Your refusal to accept responsibility and your lack of remorse only serve to underscore the depth of your depravity.

"In light of the severity of these offences, the court has no option but to impose the most severe sentence permitted by law."

Daryl's stomach churned and flipped. He couldn't bring himself to look anywhere but the floor, but, despite his averted gaze, he could feel the sting of the eyes of judgement and abhorrence stabbing into the back of his head from those in attendance.

"Mr. Jackson, I hereby sentence you to life imprisonment."

Daryl's legs buckled and he choked.

"Given the horrific nature of your crimes and your complete lack of remorse, I order that you serve a whole life term. This means you will never be eligible for parole, and you will spend the rest of your life in prison."

Murmurs and sighs rang out in the gallery as the sentence was issued.

Vomit surged in Daryl's throat and spewed from his mouth as he struggled to maintain control of his body.

"You'll fucking burn," screamed a voice from behind his quivering body.

"You inhuman piece of shit," rallied another.

The judge, visibly frustrated with the lack of decorum, hammered his gavel against the bench. "Order. Order."

An ominous hush fell across the courtroom as Daryl spat out remnants of vomit. He could hear only his own panting breaths and the drum of his heart beating out of his ribcage.

"Take him down."

Prison guards gathered around Daryl, pulled him to his feet and began ushering him away. As he was being pulled he didn't resist, but turned to face the gallery, finally laying eyes on the weeping families of those he'd hurt beyond belief.

As those eyes fell upon him he stared back with an iciness that echoed the frigidity of his soul.

* * *

20/02/1973

Daryl sat on his saggy mattress in his one-man cell. The springs had seen better days; some of them — broken and stretched — protruded through the fabric and prodded at his flesh.

His head throbbed and an icy chill filled the room.

He shuddered, got to his feet, put on a threadbare jumper and checked his reflection in the mirror above the cracked porcelain sink.

A single shard of light shone through from the tiny window above, illuminating his face.

He hardly recognised himself: his nose, disjointed; his right eye, swollen and closed up as if he'd been stung by a hornet. It was surrounded by a heavy bruise, equal parts yellow and purple.

His bottom lip was similarly bloated, but cracked and dry, leading to sporadic splits and bleeding.

A tooth was loose.

The beatings for him were common. They had started during the first week and had increased in frequency as the months passed.

Six months he'd been incarcerated.

Six months of hell on Earth.

As a convicted rapist, Daryl was the lowest of the low in here – just one step up on the ladder from the paedophiles. He counted his blessings that he'd managed to escape the rapes so far, but his stomach was constantly in knots as he feared that they would come in time.

A constant wave of dread followed him like a heavy cloud.

There was an irony in this somewhere, but he was a long way from being able to see the funny side.

The cell doors crashed open with a bang.

Breakfast time.

With a heavy head, Daryl traipsed towards the mess hall, avoiding eye contact with the other inmates and ignoring the whoops and jeers that came with the mass exodus from the cells at this time of day.

Not that you could realistically consider anyone a friend here, but Daryl had one person who was the closest thing to it – Sean.

Collecting his slop of a breakfast, Daryl scanned the hall.

There he was, in the usual spot. And he'd saved Daryl the usual seat.

Daryl sidled up to the bench and took his seat opposite Sean, placing his breakfast tray on the table.

"Thanks for saving my spot," Daryl slurred.

"No problem, pal... The eye's looking worse," Sean said, looking up from his tray, raising his eyebrows and nodding towards Daryl's swollen peeper.

"Yeah. Watcha gonna do, eh?" Daryl shovelled a forkful of grey eggs into his mouth, wincing at the sting of his cracked, bulging bottom lip.

Sean was in for murder. He'd killed his wife in a fit of rage, after finding out she was having an affair with one of his work colleagues. A crime of passion they'd called it, but it was premeditated. He'd planned it to the last detail. Tortured the poor woman.

It's funny what love can do to a man.

Sean didn't look the type. Hell, does anyone ever? A slim, well-groomed man with good teeth and a healthy crop of brown hair. Articulate. Softly spoken.

Daryl had often wondered what had caused the two of them to strike up a friendship. He'd concluded that they had three things in common: they were both in prison, they both needed someone, they'd both killed.

Desperate times – and Daryl was grateful that anyone would be willing to pass the time with a convicted rapist like him.

The old adage rang true: beggars can't be choosers.

"Those same guys putting the beatings on you?"

"Yeah," said Daryl, with a sigh of resignation. "Always the same. Those fuckers won't leave me alone. I'm forever looking over my shoulder in here."

"You ever think about fighting back?"

Daryl shook his head; so slowly it was almost unnoticeable. "That would be suicide," he muttered, looking back down at his tray and feeding himself another mouthful of unidentifiable sustenance.

"Would that be such a bad thing?"

"Huh?" Daryl's eyes flicked upwards to meet Sean's gaze.

"You're in here for life, right? You're never gonna see the outside world again. What makes you keep going?"

Sean's words hit hard. Daryl had often reflected on his situation and wondered if death would be better than this pitiful existence.

"The survival instinct is stronger than I'd ever given it credit for."

"How long might that last?" said Sean, stirring his eggs with his fork.

I question that daily.

"You want to see me killed, mate?" 'Mate' was a strong word, but it spilled from Daryl's mouth almost instinctively.

"Oh no... I'm not saying that. I'm just questioning whether that resolve will wear thin at some point. You... you need to find a way to live a bit more peacefully in here."

"I don't think peace is something you find in here."

Sean sat pensive for a few moments before responding.

"I disagree. Look around."

Daryl scanned the hall. He was first drawn to the generic, stern-faced, scowling, prison guards, but then glanced from table to table. There were some inmates sharing a familiar look of indignation; one that he could relate to, but a further examination opened his eyes to the variety on display.

A few tables over there were a group of inmates laughing and joking with each other. Heavy clangs rang out as they rapped the table in hysterics.

Smiles...

In the far corner one prisoner entered the hall, his eyes lighting up as another stood to greet him. They high-fived, shared a secret handshake and embraced.

Something stirred in Daryl's gut.

Envy?

He let out a bitter laugh.

"You see it?" said Sean, breaking the silence.

"Yeah. I see it. It's alright for some."

I'll never have that life here. I don't deserve it. A rapist will never get the respect they crave. I know my place.

"I know my place," Daryl sighed, his inner thoughts spilling out, as he turned his attention back to his grey eggs.

"It's possible," said Sean, as he gave a nod and a smile to someone from across the hall. "I know my place in here, too, man. I'll never be popular, but I live quite easily. Quite comfortably."

"Good for you."

Sean's eyes narrowed. His brow furrowed.

"What do you mean by that?"

Daryl's chest tightened.

"Shit, man. I didn't mean it like that. I'm glad I have you as a friend. And I'm... I'm pleased that you can find it... comfortable in here. Honest. I just doubt I ever will."

As Daryl uttered these words his eyes met an all too familiar stare from across the hall. He trembled as the gaze landed upon him. His pulse quickened and his palms began to sweat as the man who had orchestrated beatings upon him countless times came into view.

Harry.

Daryl's swollen eye throbbed from the memory of the last punch he had received.

Harry pointed at his own eyes and then at Daryl's.

Daggers.

Daryl shuddered. The intimidation, triggering a conditioned response. He looked away. Bowed his head.

* * *

CHAPTER 6

18/08/1973

If it wasn't for the chain-link fences and the guards on patrol, this could have been a typical summer's day stroll in the park. Daryl paced around the yard as the sun beat down on his bony frame, his grubby plimsolls kicking up dust and fag ends.

He was granted one hour a day in the yard, and this hour was the closest he got to anything resembling freedom. On a day like today, where the sky was a cerulean blue, life felt almost worthwhile.

Daryl took a deep breath and wheezed – the bruises on his ribs making it hard to inhale fully.

The grating sound of gates opening ushered in more inmates to the yard and Daryl instantly clocked Sean. He ambled in his direction and met him halfway.

"Smoke?" said Sean, offering Daryl a cigarette.

"Read my mind," he replied, taking one from Sean's exposed pack. They both lit up and sauntered around the yard.

As Daryl took a deep drag he winced.

"Fresh bruises?"

"Nothing I can't handle," said Daryl, dismissing Sean's question with a wave of his hand. "Do you know the date?"

"Eighteenth of August, I believe."

"Yeah, that's what I thought. It's hard to keep track of days in here sometimes." Daryl looked up to the sky. "One year," he sighed.

"Huh?"

"It's one year since I got thrown in here."

Daryl noticed confusion in Sean's eyes – not from the simplicity of the words, but at how to respond. There was no good response that anyone could give to this situation.

"Oh... Happy anniversary."

Isn't it just?

"Gee. Thanks," Daryl said. A bitter smile crossing his lips, He looked back to the sky as they continued to walk the short circuit around the yard.

Leaving the yard and heading back inside, Daryl was escorted to the workshop. Part of life at the prison was to have a vocation of sorts and he worked a couple of times a week on building furniture that was sold to third parties on the outside. The wages were minimal, but it kept him well stocked with cigarettes, toothpaste and other essentials. Plus, the distraction from his heavy mind was appreciated.

Daryl's nerves were more on edge these days when he entered the workshop as Harry and some of his 'associates' had also recently embarked on working in this area of the prison.

Today was no different.

There was also a dearth of prison guards in this area. No watchful eyes, but also no safety net.

Daryl kept his head down, sawing off bits of timber to size, drilling countersunk screw holes and piecing things together. He had a methodical approach. Paying delicate attention to each detail.

Mindful.

This habitual way he went about his work kept his mind quiet and the nerves to a minimum, but these days, whenever there was a loud bang or clang in the background he jumped like a scared cat.

Laughter erupted behind him.

Not laughter that was full of heart.

Laughter with a sinister edge.

Laughter directed *at* him.

Harry.

Daryl tried his best to ignore it – focusing instead on screwing planes of wood together with precision.

Footsteps approached. The sound of heavy boots on the concrete floor shattering Daryl's concentration. His mouth went dry and his heart started to beat a little faster. A little louder.

"Now what the fuck do we have here?" Harry sneered, as he grabbed hold of Daryl's construction, snatching it from his weak grip.

I can't get a minute's peace from this motherfucker.

Daryl kept his gaze on the floor.

Accompanied by two of his goons – one on either side – Harry stood directly in front of Daryl. Although he wasn't looking at them he knew who the other two were. Recognised their shoes. The sound of their laughter, familiar.

"Give it back," Daryl whispered.

"I can't hear you," said Harry, kneeling down to level himself with Daryl.

Daryl gritted his teeth, lifted his gaze to meet Harry's threatening eyes.

Like Sean said, you've got to stick up for yourself some time.

"I said. Give it the fuck back!"

The laughter from Harry's sidekicks ceased momentarily and Daryl got to his feet with an urgency and intent that surprised him.

Harry rose in tandem.

Eye to eye.

Daryl glanced at the men positioned either side of Harry. One, a scrawny man, a couple of inches shorter than Harry with faint wisps of hair on his head. The other – broader – but still a shadow of Harry, with a tattoo on his neck of a love heart with 'Mum' emblazoned in the centre.

Sweet.

"What the fuck you gonna do about it?" Harry pressed.

What I should have done a long time ago.

The rage spilt over. The built up anger that had been brewing for the last year couldn't be contained any longer. It drowned out any reasoning of consequence.

He didn't think twice.

Daryl launched a swift punch to Harry's gut, causing him to double over with a forced exhale.

A quick follow up and Daryl also caught him in the jaw with a crack, splitting Harry's lip.

Still standing, Harry blinked. Slightly dazed, but clearly unperturbed, he wiped his lip with a finger and showed the crimson soaked digit to Daryl, his eyes menacing.

Oh shit.

"You've got a bit of a spark in you all of a sudden. Don't get too excited though. Now we're gonna have to put that out." He side-eyed each of his men in turn and they reciprocated with a smile. "Hold him, boys. I'm gonna teach this fucking rapist a lesson."

Harry's men raced to grab Daryl's arms, knocking tools from a workbench in their wake with a bang. Sawdust spiralled in the air. Harry immediately followed with a heavy punch that he rammed into Daryl's gut; his already bruised ribs aflame as the wind was knocked out of him.

The punch reverberated through Daryl's torso.

He choked. Doubled over.

Daryl caught his breath and righted himself. He didn't wrestle against his restraints, but stared straight into Harry's eyes with a resolve he wasn't used to. His mouth was full of saliva from the coughing that had erupted following the hammer blow to the stomach and without thinking he spat straight into Harry's face.

His goons took an audible sharp intake of breath as Harry froze. His eyes, wide. He wiped the spit from his cheek with his palm, looked down at his hand and then at Daryl. He gave a wry smile, arched his hand back and slapped Daryl squarely on the side of the face with his spit-soaked hand emitting a thunder clap.

The crack of the slap caused Daryl's ears to ring and his head to spin. He saw stars. He blinked to clear his vision and took a breath, his throbbing ribs causing him to wince. He made a concerted and conscious effort to hide his discomfort and stared back into Harry's eyes again.

Defiant.

Harry's expression turned from a smile to a scowl. His eyes narrowed.

"Right, boys. Get him down on the floor. Face down." His sidekicks looked at Harry with a reservation that Daryl hadn't seen from them until now. Their eyebrows arched. Their eyes wide. With.... *fear*? "Now!"

His men hesitated, but Harry's menacing stare won out and they began wrestling Daryl to the floor.

Daryl tried to resist the restraint, to which Harry issued another blow to his burning stomach giving him no chance to stop the inevitable.

He was on the ground now; his face, breathing sawdust, as he struggled against his assailants.

Fear was starting to swell within Daryl in his now helpless

state and as Harry's goons held him pinned against the sawdust-covered, concrete floor, Harry reached underneath him and pulled down his trousers.

"You spit in my face. I'm gonna teach you a fucking lesson," slurred Harry. His voice, almost demonic.

The silence in the workshop rang heavy. No one else was present. No one else to step in. No one to stop what was coming.

The only sounds – Daryl's own panting, his timpani drum of a heartbeat, the goons heavy breaths.

And then, the ominous sound of Harry undoing his own belt buckle.

Harry's face came in close to Daryl's now. His breath, hot and hoarse in his ear. "You think you can spit in my face and get away with it. It's time for your lesson, rapist."

Daryl continued to wrestle against the three of them with futility and as Harry thrust himself inside, Daryl let out a whimper.

Pain swelled and seared, and with each thrust, Daryl relented a little more. His eyes glazed over as Harry continued to deliver his punishment.

It could have been seconds, or minutes, but Daryl had no earthly idea. He'd detached from his reality; hadn't been consciously present for the ordeal. His mind had shut off and forced him to disassociate from the harsh truth of what was happening to him.

Awareness only came once he heard the footsteps of three men recede accompanied by no words.

Daryl sat foetal on the floor of the shower block, obscured by the steam from the hot water that rained on his shaking body.

With his head bowed he looked on as blood ran from between his legs, mixed with the shower water and whirled and spiralled down the plughole.

He convulsed as he sobbed uncontrollably.

He slapped his face repeatedly as he chastised himself.

"Get a grip, you idiot."

"You had this coming."

His words echoed against the ceramic tiles of the shower enclosure and as he lowered his tone to a whisper waves of regret and shame swelled within him.

"You've done worse to others."

Happy anniversary.

* * *

20/11/1973

The days grew darker. Not just in terms of daylight hours, but also in Daryl's soul.

Following his sexual assault at the hands of Harry, he'd become more withdrawn and kept his time spent outside of his cell to a minimum. He'd ditched tinkering away at the workshop; couldn't face the place. And he also spent less than the approved hour in the yard.

The frequent beatings had seemingly ceased and the ominous, oppressive figure of Harry had changed. *He* now walked alone, too; his usual swagger replaced with an amble. When they had crossed paths, Daryl had tended to keep his head down, but on the one occasion that their eyes had met he had noticed something different about that stare. Less menacing. More subdued. Distant. Something that mirrored Daryl's own gaze.

Shame.

Makes sense.

You've become the thing you despised in me. Welcome to the despicable club.

In his cell, Daryl gripped the sink and stared in the mirror. The reflection that greeted him was that of a stranger. No bruises were on show, but his expression said more than a hundred bruises ever could. His face was ashen. His eyes, hollow. His hair, starting to grey.

As he stared, he thought of his past.

The harsh reality hit him like one of Harry's punches. For the first time he truly understood what he had done.

The brutal, senseless, rape and murder that he'd inflicted on those poor women screamed into his psyche.

Flashes of their horrified expressions erupted in his mind's eye.

Hallucinatory echoes of their screams.

What I put them through is unforgivable.

I know how it feels to be raped and humiliated now.

I only wish I'd been killed, too.

Ashamed of the man that stared back, he turned his face away from the mirror.

* * *

03/02/1974

The winter had been brutal. Daryl clutched his bedsheets and pulled them up to his chin. He shivered, even though he was fully clothed beneath the covers.

He couldn't sleep; haunted by a perfect storm of deterrents: the bitter cold, the clanging and hollering of the other inmates along the row, the constant throbbing of his brain reminding him of the suffering he'd caused and, most significantly, the black cloud of depression that followed his every move and refused to budge to let any light into his life at all.

Still wide awake as the cell doors banged open, Daryl got to his feet and trudged wearily to the mess hall. He collected his meal with no words exchanged and sat at an empty seat, staring down at his food with an absence of interest.

His appetite these days was limited to an absolute bare minimum and his skeletal frame echoed this fact. His body was gaunt, his cheeks hollow and his eyes were sunken deep into his skull.

Those eyes.

They sat heavy on his face.

A great weight of sadness beneath them.

The dark passenger. Depression. It had claimed him fully now. It weighed down every thought and breath. He had tried to dismiss it as being simply a symptom of the cold, dreary winter days, but it was so much more than that.

It was a diminishing of his soul.

A tormentor that would beat him down and destroy any vibrancy that was left of his life.

A chair squeaked opposite.

Keeping his head down, Daryl raised his eyes to see a familiar face.

"I saved you a spot," said Sean. "Why don't you ever join me nowadays?"

Daryl looked back down; scraped his fork along his tray.

"I haven't seen you for what feels like an age," Sean continued.

Daryl merely grunted. Took a sip of water.

"How have things been? You don't seem to have any war wounds, so that's good, eh?"

Daryl tutted and rolled his eyes, out of view of Sean. He placed a fork with the merest of morsels loaded upon it to his lips and wrestled with swallowing it.

"I'll be honest, mate. You don't look good and I can see you're struggling to eat. Is there anything you want to talk about?"

Daryl continued to roll food around his dry mouth. Finally swallowing the meagre portion, he said, "No," a croak to his voice.

Sean leaned forward, rested his hands on the table so that they came into view of Daryl's lowered gaze.

"I know..." Sean's voice cracked. "I know what... happened."

Daryl's fork clattered to the table and he looked up to meet Sean's gaze, his eyes red and moist.

"What did you say?" Daryl's eyes narrowed as he surveyed Sean. "You know nothing about me, or what I'm going through," he growled.

Sean pulled his hands away from the table and held them up. A look of shock plastered his face at the tone of Daryl's response.

"Hey, man... I didn't mean anything by it. I'm sorry... I didn't want to assume... I don't know... Shit, man. It's just..." Sean lowered his tone to a whisper. "But I know about—"

"Shut the fuck up."

Daryl felt a surge of rage build inside him and he pushed his tray forward with such force that it upended. Food remnants went flying into Sean's chest.

Sean was left stunned. His mouth hung open, but no words followed.

The room was filled with murmurs and groans, but these were muted by Daryl's black cloud that shrouded him. He thrust himself to his feet, gave Sean a stern stare, turned and walked away; his heavy steps leading him back to his cell.

* * *

??/??/1976

The days rolled on. Things remained the same. Except for the fact that he now had no one to confide in. No one to talk to since his outburst at Sean.

Even if he did want to talk to or confide in Sean, that ship had sailed. He'd moved on. He ignored Daryl now and would sit in a different part of the mess hall with different inmates; would strut the yard with a different tribe.

That's right. Plural.

Daryl would give the occasional glance over at Sean in the mess hall and see him laughing and joking with others, while he sat alone. A gnawing feeling would hit him in the pit of his stomach, twisting and turning like a knife digging deep into his soul and he'd simply look away, focus on the bleak, empty space in front of him and his own solitude.

How long had it been since his outburst at Sean? Maybe two years, although it was hard to tell. Time seemed to move differently when you didn't have anyone to talk to and Daryl couldn't remember the last time he uttered any words.

As he sat on a bench in the yard, scraping his feet in the gravel and dust, he spied Sean kicking a football around with four other prisoners. They would pass to each other, do some kick-ups, header it between them and try and volley into a goal that they'd crudely assembled with a pack of cigarettes marking each goal post.

The laughter and hollering that echoed and danced in the air from the five of them shook through Daryl.

I could have been a part of that.

My days could have been easier.

Daryl averted his gaze. Looked down at his feet.

As he sat, the football came rolling over and bounced off Daryl's idle foot with a dull thud. He heard quick steps running towards him and raised his eyes to see Sean reaching for the ball.

As he scooped it up, there was a split-second before he turned away to jog back to the others, where his eyes met Daryl's.

Time stopped.

That split-second felt like minutes.

A sea of unspoken words. Essays could have been written about that look they shared.

Sean's eyes had a vibrancy. A life. But once they'd clocked Daryl there was an instant switch to one of resentment. Not just resentment. Pity.

Daryl's eyes on the contrary were void of life. Vacant.

At that moment, Daryl wanted to say something – wanted his

vocal chords to spark to life for the first time in two years.

But he had no words.

His chance came and went in that split-second as Sean looked from Daryl's eyes, to the ground, followed by the briefest of hesitations before he turned and wheeled away with the ball in his hands.

A tightness welled in Daryl's chest.

I could have simply said, I'm sorry.

Would that have been enough?

A tear formed in Daryl's pained eyes.

The hollers continued and Daryl remained sitting alone with only his remorseful thoughts for company; a single tear inching down his pale cheek.

* * *

??/??/????

Dawn would turn to dusk and dusk to dawn. The meaningless cycle of days and nights.

By now, Daryl had completely lost track of the essence of time and had no earthly idea of what year it was, let alone what day or month. He could only hazard a guess at it being some time in winter based on how bitterly cold it had been and how short the daylight hours had become.

The knowledge of how many years he'd been imprisoned escaped him. It must have been at least ten. Prison time could be marked by the comings and goings of inmates and the recent staggering news that Sean had been released hit home the extent of the time Daryl must have served.

The revelation haunted him.

The one person who had seemed like a friend in here. Gone. And Daryl held a heavy amount of regret for the fact that his own self pity had been the cause for this one and only connection slipping through his grasp.

He wondered how Sean was adapting to life back on the outside and a pang of jealousy swelled in his gut at the thought of it.

What are you doing right now, Sean?

Do you have a girl?

Do you have friends out there?

Daryl was paralysed by grief. It burnt. A heavy sorrow for losing out on a life that he would never get to live. It only went to exacerbate the effects of the deep depression he was suffering from and he'd now reached a point where he was beyond caring about time passing.

What difference does it make? One way or another, I'm gonna die in here.

As Daryl sat on his bed in his cramped, lonely cell, he watched as the setting sun painted shadows on the floor; casting an imprint of the bars from his letterbox of a window above. Shadows that gradually crept up the wall in front of him.

An eerie sundial.

He rocked forwards and pushed himself up from the edge of the bed and moved to the sink in the corner. More cracks were exposed on the porcelain these days. Much like you could tell a tree's age by its rings, Daryl's sink showed its age through a network of fractures in its now weak structure.

The sink wasn't the only thing showing its age in this cell. Daryl splashed some water on his face and stared hard at his reflection in the mirror above.

What he saw staring back shocked him.

He hadn't looked at himself in what felt like an eternity and the face looking back was a generation removed from his memory. Deep wrinkles lined his brow; pronounced crow's feet cracked the corners of his eyes. His cheeks were hollow and pale; his hair almost entirely grey and thinning. Heavy bags sagged beneath his eyes.

And those eyes.

Empty.

He had entered prison as a relatively young man. The reflection was that of an elderly stranger.

Haunted by his own appearance, Daryl turned away and sat back on the bed. As he fell onto the ragged mattress another broken spring sprang through the fabric and poked him in his skinny thigh. He winced and grabbed hold of the metal protrusion; pulling it hard and fast and yanking it out of the mattress, tearing a strip of fabric in its wake.

Frustration surged in Daryl's stomach. His pale face turned red with angst and he tore at other exposed springs and wrenched them free, turning his aged mattress into ribbons.

The rage grew with each tear of the mattress and he didn't stop until it had become an unrecognisable heap of shredded fabric and bent springs.

He sat in a ball on the floor of his cell – panting, as he looked at the chaotic mess he'd created. His hands, trembling.

The sudden pause that came following the destruction caused a surge of emotion within him that he was powerless to stop.

He wept.

For the lives he'd taken.

For his life that had been taken.

As he sat there, crumpled on the floor – his face, wet – a thought occurred to him.

He tried to shake it from his mind, but it burrowed deeper.

A call to action.

He got to his feet, leaned over the butchered mattress, heaped up the torn material and began tying strips of fabric together. He hooked one end through the bars of his small window and secured it with a tight knot.

At the other end he fashioned a loop.

He stood on the edge of his exposed metal bed frame, placed his head through that loop and teetered on the edge.

He rocked back and forth.

He hesitated.

Once.

Twice.

Then pushed away.

I'm sorry.

The crude noose grew taut.

His body convulsed for a few agonising seconds before he went limp.

The setting sun cast a shadow of his lifeless body on the wall of his cell.

That shadow swung like a pendulum.

Chapter 7

I was found on the floor.

My body being shaken brought me to my senses.

I choked and instinctively clawed at my neck to pull at the noose. Loosen its grip.

But there was no noose to be found.

I felt wet.

I blinked my eyes open. Squinted at the brightness of the lights around me.

My vision was blurred. I saw stars – behind them I could make out a shape I believed to be a face, but I couldn't bring it into focus. Unreachable.

I was vacant for a moment. A fog clouding my senses.

I shook my head and with a spark of clarity, I spoke.

I hadn't spoken words for years.

"Where am I?"

I was surprised that the words came easy. No croak to my voice. But yet, it sounded unfamiliar.

"Julius. You're safe."

Julius?

My vision sharpened. The stars cleared.

I focused on the face in front of me. I had a sense that I knew it

– but from a distant memory. Like a memory of another lifetime.

"Who are you?" I said, narrowing my eyes, as I scrutinised the face looking down at me.

"Mensch. I'm your friend, Mensch."

Mensch?

The name resonated, but it felt like a name from a dream I'd had; not someone I knew consciously.

My head rattled.

"Why do I feel wet?"

Mensch looked down at my legs. "That's you. You did that to yourself."

"What does that mean?" I said. I couldn't make sense of those words.

"Do I need to spell it out for you? You... you've pissed yourself."

My head span.

"What the hell? Where is this? Why am I not in my cell?"

Mensch looked confused.

"What do you think your name is?"

I must have mirrored Mensch's expression. Confusion was taking hold of me, too. This exchange seemed surreal. Dream-like.

"What do I *think* my name is? I don't need to *think*. I *know*. I'm Daryl."

"Daryl?"

"Yes! And where the fuck *am* I?"

I attempted to scramble to my feet, but a wave of dizziness hit me and I instead fell into a crumpled heap on the floor. I touched my crotch and felt the wetness of my urine-soaked trousers.

Propping myself up onto my elbows, I stared around the room – it clearly wasn't my cell. Bright fluorescent lights above me burnt my retinas. A low grade hum echoed and filled the air with an ambient buzz. Screens with indiscernible symbols and lights, that had no earthly sense in the 1970s, were paraded around my periphery. To my left, a high backed chair loomed above me. It had an air of familiarity and foreboding.

A futuristic setting.

Am I hallucinating? Is this a dream?

Am I dead?

I should be dead.

"You're home," said Mensch. "Hang on. I have something that may help."

My head throbbed; a gnawing pain beating away in a place that I couldn't touch.

Mensch trudged away and promptly returned brandishing a mirror. He passed it to me and said, "Now, just take your time. Look into this. This is the real you."

"The *real* me?" I said, as I laughed and rolled my eyes.

I raised the mirror to my face. The apparition that revealed itself made my hands shake and I dropped the mirror with a clatter. "What the fuck is this? Some kind of trick?!" I stared at Mensch with gritted teeth.

Mensch looked to the mirror and then to my eyes. He gave a nod.

There was a stillness to this man and I felt inclined to oblige with his subtle order. With trembling hands I picked up the mirror again. I raised it with hesitation; gradually bringing my face into the frame.

The hair first. A full head. Not grey.

My forehead. No clear wrinkles.

The eyes.

Eyes of a stranger.

I gulped and revealed the rest of the face to myself.

The face of a young man stared back at me.

I gasped.

The face in the mirror did the same.

"You've been in the simulation again. You're Julius."

"Simulation? Julius?" I whispered, patting my cheeks. They were smooth and taut. Unfamiliar.

Julius.

I repeated the name over and over in my mind and with each iteration a fragment of the illusion shattered. I scanned my reflection several times, casting expressions in the glass that the mirror echoed flawlessly.

Fractured memories surged from behind my mind's eye – a life in this reality, where I was this man, Julius. The year?

2132.

Not the 1970s.

What the fuck is happening?

I was silent for many minutes.

I could feel the twisting of a tangled mess of memories that had congealed in my brain and my head buzzed with the effort of trying to work through them.

It's 2132.

We live under a world of a broken sky, not the cerulean blue of the twentieth century.

A broken sky that I rarely get to see.

* * *

"So tell me. Where were you? *When* were you?" said Mensch, as he placed a steaming cup of coffee next to me.

After the minutes of heavy silence, I'd fought to regain my balance against the dizziness I was struggling with. I'd ambled back to my room to change out of my soiled clothes and then met up again with Mensch.

We now sat in the living quarters. Mensch on one sofa; me on the other.

We faced each other.

The room felt alien to me, although somewhere in the dark recesses of my brain I somehow knew it. It was homely, yet sterile.

"The nineteen seventies," I said, as I reached for the coffee. "Prison." This last word came out as a whisper and I lowered my head as I uttered it.

"Prison?" Mensch asked, clearly bewildered. "You were saying you were *Daryl?*"

"I *am* Daryl. I... I've lived more of his life than I have any–" I stumbled over my words; cut myself off, as Daryl's memories of his last moments surged inside of my addled brain. My eyes swelled.

"What did you think you were doing? Why were you down there?" I noticed a look of anger and frustration wash over Mensch's face. "Why did you enter the simulation alone? It's not supposed to be used without supervision, you know?!"

"I... I... I don't remember. It's a *lifetime* ago." I rubbed my eyes. "It was calling me."

"You were in for eight hours."

"Eight hours?" My head spun and my eyes opened wide. "What do you mean eight hours? I've spent a lifetime in prison!" My hands started to tremble and I felt a wave of sadness all of a sudden. A hopelessness. A darkness.

Daryl's hopelessness.

Daryl's darkness.

"I'm sorry, Julius."

Julius.

"Stop calling me Julius for fuck's sake. I can barely remember him." A lump was lodged in my throat and a tear formed – I couldn't quite understand why.

Mensch leaned forward. Rested his head on his hands.

"That must have been awful. Can you... can you tell me any more about Daryl? About your *experience*?"

"I'll tell you," I said, a rasp to my voice. "I'm a rapist. I was sentenced to life for raping and killing four women. How's that for a fucking experience."

The tear dripped down my cheek and fell into the cup of coffee I cradled, creating ripples on the surface.

"A rapist?" Mensch gulped. He was clearly shocked, but was trying his best to display a calm demeanour.

"Yes! And I've spent the last few decades living with that fucking truth."

A sudden surge of rage erupted inside me. I screamed and threw my cup at the wall. Coffee erupted and splattered on the wall and the floor, as the cup smashed into a thousand pieces with a crash that echoed within the confines of these four walls.

Mensch sat bolt upright; a look of visceral terror painted his face, and as I watched the transition in Mensch's expression, a thought occurred to me:

You may have known me before, but you don't know me now.

"This is dangerous, Julius."

"Stop it with the Julius references," I shouted.

"I'm shutting down the programme."

"What do you mean?" I said, lowering my tone and meeting

Mensch's stare with wild eyes.

"The simulation. It's clearly dangerous. Look at what it's done to you."

"Is this a surprise to you? I'm not the only one, surely? What's it done to the others?"

Mensch's face turned a shade of red. He slumped in his seat.

Something's wrong here.

"What are you not telling me?"

I saw his hands tremble. He opened his mouth, but no words came.

"What is it?!"

"Ok... just stay calm, ok?"

"*Stay calm*? Tell me!"

Mensch fidgeted with his hands. A sweat had broken out on his brow.

"You were the first," he whispered.

My stomach flipped. My legs went numb.

"What? That's not true."

"I'm sorry."

"But... but... I'm sure I remember others telling me about their experiences. About how life changing it was."

"I'm sorry. They were just telling you what you wanted to hear." Mensch's hands were visibly shaking, as was his voice. "To... to get you to go along with it," he said, hurrying through the last of these words.

I choked; doubled over and threw up on the steel floor beneath me.

"What?" I gagged, the acrid smell of vomit ablaze in my nostrils.

"I'm sorry. You were the trial run. I... I... I should've–"

What the fuck?

Mensch's revelation carved into me. Rage surged. The nausea, forgotten. I cut him off from having a chance at dealing me any pathetic excuses and fired back at him in a torrent of fury.

"And you let me try this out and find out for myself how much it can fuck with your head?! Do you realise what I am now?! I'm not a single person anymore, Mensch, you fucking cunt." Hunter's words. "I'm *four* fucking people... and the one that seems to be taking ownership of me right now... the one I resonate with the most is... Daryl – the one whose life I've actively lived the longest. The one who was enduring life time imprisonment. The one who was subjected to frequent beatings and rape. And fuck, what am I *saying*? It was me! I *am* Daryl. *I* experienced those things! *I* was beaten. *I* was raped. And now those memories... They've followed me home! To *this* life. Where I am apparently *Julius*."

I took a breath, spat out some remnants of vomit and carried on. "Whoever this Julius is, I'm less him than I've ever been... And I have to live with that." My eyes started to fill with tears and my voice started to tremble. "I have to live with Daryl's awful, pathetic, desperate life... *My* life."

I began sobbing.

"I have his scars. Maybe not physically. But mentally." Tears dropped and my body shook. "I feel them. My soul. It is what I am."

Seconds passed. No words from either of us. I searched Mensch's face for answers. None were found. I stared at him with pleading eyes.

I tried to get away from the grave reality of the situation – tried to access Hayden's memories. The best time of my life. The most free I'd ever felt. They were still there somewhere; buried in my addled brain, but they were harder to reach.

Daryl's memories now took centre stage.

"It's ok. You're safe now. You're *home*," said Mensch. There was an irony to his words.

My hands scrunched into fists. My nails dug into my palms.

"Safe? *SAFE?!* How can I be fucking safe when my mind is not my own. I'm a fucking rapist! A murderer. A convicted prisoner. A low life fucking scumbag."

My voice was growing hoarse from my ragged screams.

"You're none of those things. You're Julius."

"My memories tell me otherwise. What are we if not our experiences and our memories. I'm more Daryl than Julius. I've lived more of his life than my own. It may have been only a matter of a few hours in *this* reality, but as far as my mind knows it was pretty much a lifetime.

"I died in that prison at my own hand. Depression and hopelessness killed me. And it's followed me back. It's part of me now. And. That. Is. My. *Reality*!"

Mensch was shaken. I hadn't noticed during my outburst, but he had moved to stand behind the sofa; shielding himself from me. Clearly worried that I may lash out at him.

Mensch raised his hands in surrender as he finally uttered, "You will be fine, though. Those memories will fade. Just like the last time. You slept it off. *Remember*? And you returned to being just Julius."

No. They won't.

"I lied about that," I whispered. A rasp to my voice.

"What?" Mensch lowered his hands; terror littered his face.

"They didn't fade. They... they stuck with me," I said, as I raised my eyebrows, my forehead creasing. "I'm still partly Hayden. Partly Hunter. But now I'm more Daryl than anyone. And Daryl's black cloud has followed me home."

I feel your depression, Daryl.

I am *you.*

I cannot escape this truth.

A silence hung in the air; as heavy as the weight of Daryl's past pressing down on me.

Mensch stood. Unmoving. His mouth hung open, but no words left his lips. There was nothing he could say. Nothing that could change the truth of what I had become.

You can dismantle the program.

But for me the simulation won't be over. It never can be.

It's done its damage.

I am Daryl's dark cloud.

I couldn't face Mensch any longer. I needed to get out of this room. Needed some air. I stormed out and sprinted to the bathroom.

I barged through the door, grasped hold of the sink and looked down at the plughole, panting.

A familiar pose.

My head pounded. Throbbed.

A million memories swarmed. Mainly Daryl's.

I took a couple of deep breaths and raised my gaze to the mirror above.

I stared at myself.

Grey, wispy hair. A sea of wrinkles. Battle scars.

A weathered face.

Daryl's face.

I screamed and punched the mirror, shattering it into a spider's web.

Pieces of broken glass clattered into the porcelain bowl below, but the majority of the mirror remained in place. Fractured.

My hand — bloodied — dripped viscous liquid into the sink and I shook from the rage that welled within. The physical outburst had done little to stem it.

I looked down into the sink again as the drops of blood from my quivering knuckles fell and painted the surface of the bowl and slid across shards of gleaming, broken glass.

I panted and searched for a calming breath, but my inhales were ragged. I clutched the edge of the sink and stared back at the mirror. The fractured remnants returned a kaleidoscope vision of a person.

Persons.

In one section I could see one of Hunter's narrow dark eyes; and some of his flowing, dark, matted hair. In another, I saw Hayden's beautiful smile. Her clear skin. Her innocence. In a third I saw one of Julius's eyes. His furrowed brow. The tiny scar above.

Lastly I rested upon a neck. An aged, wrinkled neck, complete with dark bruising.

Bruising formed from strangulation exerted by a noose.

I'm losing my mind.

I've lost *my mind.*

I couldn't look at the mirror any longer. I looked back down to the sink.

A sharp glint reflected from a hefty chunk of mirror glass that was partly coated with blood from my knuckles.

Daryl's voice erupted in my mind.

Do it.

With his black cloud in full control, I reached in and grabbed the piece of glass. I gripped it tight and winced as it cut into my palm.

I took one last glance at the mirror - a scattered and fractured monochrome image of Daryl's face stared back at me.

There's no escape.

Do it.

His heavy darkness was omnipresent, Julius was gone and I was powerless to stop Daryl's taunts.

I rammed the glass into my jugular and wrenched it towards my windpipe.

I gagged as rhythmic jets of crimson exploded onto the mirror's surface.

Chapter 8

"Julius Died."

The words echoed.

Chapter 9

I tore off my headset in frustration, removed my headphones and tossed them across the room.

"Fuck," I sighed, slumping back into the sofa.

Footsteps approached and my roommate appeared in the doorway, grinning.

"That game again?" he asked, already knowing the answer. "You know it's more a simulation of human instinct than a game, right? You have about as much control as a gambler-holic in a casino." He chuckled to himself. "Let me guess—Julius got hooked again?"

"Happens every time."

"You can't fight fate."

"Yeah, maybe. But this time it was brutal. He ended up in prison, serving a life sentence as a rapist."

"Woah. Did he get out?"

"No," I said flatly, shaking my head. "He killed himself."

"Jeez. That's dark. Remind me... what happened last time?"

"His head imploded. Too many memories packed into his brain."

"Ah, yeah, that's right." He laughed. "You ever see that movie *WarGames*?"

"Not in ages. Why?"

"Like Joshua says, 'The only winning move is not to play.'"

I laughed. "Yeah, it seems that way, but, man, this game is so fucking good. It's so *real*. By far the most sophisticated game there's ever been. I'm hooked." I sighed. "I can't stop."

"Maybe you should," he said, disappearing into the kitchen.

He was right. I needed a break. Some air.

Prising myself from the sofa, I got to my feet. My legs were heavy, like I hadn't used them in days.

Out on the balcony, the cool night breeze hit my face. I exhaled, watching as my breath clouded in the air and disappeared into the darkness.

Julius's journey stuck with me as I stared into the night sky. His torment and seemingly unavoidable demise gnawed away at me. His sadness felt too real, like he was more than pixels and code.

He's only a character in a game. Get over it.

The thought, however accurate, didn't sit right with me.

I lit a cigarette and looked up at the stars, as if they held answers.

Julius thought *he* was real.

He thought *he* was the one playing. Watching.

But he wasn't. He was in *my* game.

So how could I be sure I wasn't in someone else's?

My stomach flipped.

What if someone is controlling me right now? What if free will is an illusion? What if someone is watching me, feeling my every sensation?

I looked down at my fingers, tracing the whorls of my fingerprints. Unique, apparently.

I touched my fingers together and felt the spark of sensation.

It felt real.

But how can I know?

The thoughts kept coming like a flood. An unanswerable onslaught.

What is reality?

Do I exist?

And if I don't...

Does it matter?

I dropped my cigarette to the floor, crushed it underfoot, the ember extinguishing in a tiny puff of smoke.

I need to stop playing that fucking game.

I gazed up at the two moons, hanging silently in the night sky.